Hector's Escapades

Hector's Escapades
The First Night Out

Text by
Jane Scoggins Bauld

Illustrated by
Gary Laronde

EAKIN PRESS ★ AUSTIN, TX

FIRST EDITION

Copyright © 1998
By Jane Scoggins Bauld

Published in the United States of America
By Eakin Press
A Division of Sunbelt Media, Inc.
P.O. Box 90159
Austin, TX 78709
email: eakinpub@sig.net

2 3 4 5 6 7 8 9

ISBN 1-57168-244-9

Library of Congress Cataloging-in-Publication Data

Bauld, Jane Scoggins.
Hector's escapades / written by Jane Scoggins Bauld.
    p.   cm.
  Summary: Hector, a Mexican free-tailed bat, spends the summer in Austin, Texas, before migrating for the winter to Mexico.
  ISBN 1-57168-244-9
  [1. Mexican free-tailed bat--Fiction. 2. Bats--Fiction 3. Austin (Tex.)--Fiction.] I. Title
pioneer life--Texas--Sources. 3. Clarksville (Tex.)--History-
PZ7.B3265He 1997
[E]--dc21   97-32037
                                            CIP
                                            AC

This book is dedicated with love to all the children of Austin, where I have taught for the past thirty years.
Jane Scoggins Bauld

For Minnie, my wife, and our boys, Brandon and Shane.
Gary Laronde

About the Bats

One of the largest bat colonies in North America lives in Austin, Texas. During the summer months, the Mexican Free Tailed bats live under Congress Avenue Bridge. They spend the winter months living in caves of Central Mexico, then migrate back to Texas for the warm summer.

Some bat colonies, such as the one in Austin, are nursery colonies. Most of the bats are female. Soon after her arrival, the female gives birth to one bat pup.

In five weeks the pup learns to fly and leaves the bridge with his mother each evening.

This is the story of one of those pups.

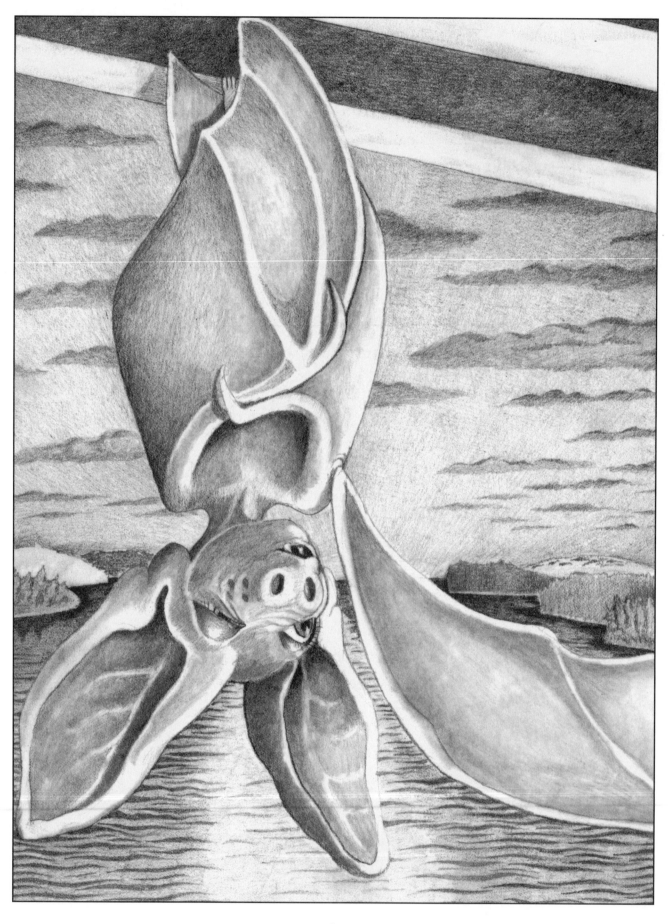

The evening started off as usual, with one more little "bat nap." Hector felt his mother nudge him with her long wing.

"Time to wake up, Hector. Time for you to learn to fly. Wake up, Hector."

Hector yawned sleepily. He opened one eye and saw that day was turning to night. The sun was disappearing behind the distant hills.

In another few moments it would be dark.

Darkness is the time the bats come out. After sleeping all day, Hector and his mother were hungry.

And Hector was excited.

This was his first night out! "What if I can't fly? What if I can't catch bugs?" Hector worried.

"Come on, Hector. Stretch your wings, like this...Now, let's go!"

Releasing the hold from his roosting place, Hector and his mother swooped down — then up, up, into the sky.

Away they flew into the darkening sky.

"I *can* fly! I *can* fly! Hooray!" shouted Hector gleefully.

Hector's roost was not the usual cave. It was a bridge!

People were standing on the bridge, watching the bats fly out. "What are they doing, Mother?" he asked.

"Oh, never mind the people, Hector. They just like to watch the bats fly out. Just stay away from them and they won't bother you," she reassured him.

So there they were, watching the bats flutter into the sky like a long, black ribbon.

The air was filled with sounds of the bats as they twittered back and forth to each other. Their echoing sounds kept them from bumping into each other.

Little by little, the bats separated into small groups. Each group went its own way, to favorite bug-hunting spots.

Hector and his mother headed for the bright lights of Disch Falk Field.

The baseball game was just starting. Hector's mother knew there was plenty of time to devour the juicy bugs attracted to the lights.

Hector lost all track of time. It was his first time to eat a bug. He and his mother ate and ate and ate.

"I *can* catch bugs! Hooray!" Hector shouted.

The moths tasted especially delicious to him!

While the baseball game continued below, the bats happily munched bugs up above.

It was about this time that Hector felt daring. He decided to venture off on his own, away from his mother.

Now, he had never left his mother's side before. But while she was turned the other way, off he went, fluttering and twittering.

Hooray! He was off on his own in the warm summer evening. What an adventure!

How far he flew, he didn't know. What he *did* know was that when he turned to go back to the baseball field, he couldn't find it.

Search as he might, he could not find the bright lights of the field. How could he have known that the baseball game would end, and the lights would be turned off?

"Oh, no!" Hector exclaimed. "I'm lost." He was scared, and he knew his mother would be worried about him.

He flew in one direction for a while, but it began to feel wrong. He turned in the other direction, but it soon began to feel wrong too.

"I'm completely lost!" he said dejectedly.

He could find nothing that looked familiar.

He could not hear the sounds of any of the bat family who had left the bridge with him. What had happened to all the other bats?

Why had he wandered away from his mother?

Would he ever be able to find his way home to the Congress Avenue Bridge?

"The bridge! That's it! I'll look for the river," Hector thought.

With great effort, he flew as fast as he could fly.

His mother had warned him about owls. "Owls fly at night looking for food too," she cautioned him. "But owls like to eat BATS! So watch out."

Hector looked about furtively. His mother had told him to find a tree branch if he ever saw an owl. The branch would help hide him.

By now it was almost dawn, and Hector was getting sleepier by the minute. He knew that soon he *must* find a place to sleep.

How he longed to be in his roost under the bridge. How he longed to hear his mother's voice.

A large tree caught Hector's eye. He flew down to the tree cautiously. It *looked* safe enough.

He hung on to a sturdy branch and swung upside down. With a soft sigh of loneliness, he drew his wings close to his body, and in less than a minute he was asleep.

As Hector slept, he began to dream. He dreamed that he was asleep under the bridge beside his mother. In his dream he could even feel her warm body beside him.

He felt her nudge him with her wing.

That was when he felt the first POKE.

POKE!

POKE!

He didn't know how long he had been sleeping.

POKE! There came another one, then another, even harder. Something was poking him with a stick.

Hector opened his eyes and saw two little boys below, poking him with a long stick. They didn't even know what he was. They were calling him a mouse.

"A mouse!" thought Hector. "Don't they know a mouse can't fly!"

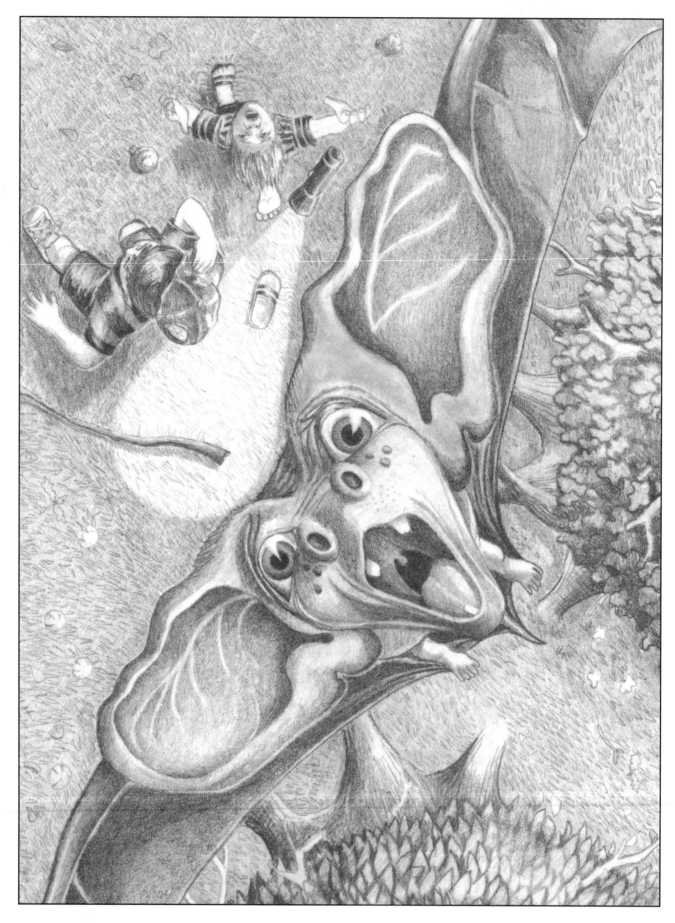

Hector knew he had to get out of there fast. He opened his wings to fly out of the tree. At his first movement, the boys shrieked at the top of their lungs and jumped back.

"It's a vampire bat! Run for your life," they yelled.

"Vampire," echoed Hector. "Don't they know vampire bats only live in the tropics? I'm not a vampire. I don't live on blood, I live on insects!"

Frantically, Hector flew. He closed his eyes and pretended he was near the bridge. That felt better.

He listened for echo sounds.

On he flew, not knowing where, but knowing that he had to keep flying.

All of a sudden he heard a familiar sound. It was the vibrating sound of another bat in flight. He headed toward the sound.

Then he heard something that made his little bat heart leap with joy. He heard a voice calling, "Hector . . . Hector." It was his mother's voice!

"Follow me home, Hector."

Hector followed closely, very closely, all the way.

Soon he smelled the old familiar smells as they swooped down to their very own place under the bridge. The cool air of the river soothed Hector's tired body.

Above the bridge, the day was turning sunny. Busy people came and went across the bridge. But for Hector, under the bridge, it was dark and still.

He hung beside his mother and soon was deep, deep in sleep.

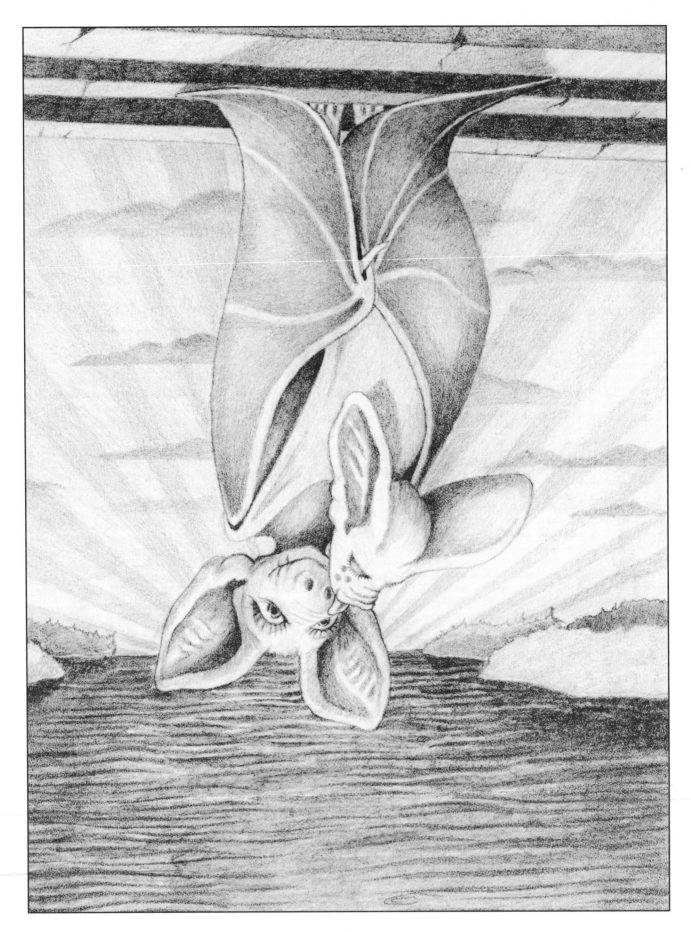

Hector knew that his mother would wake him at dusk. Together they would again go out into the night to search for insects.

This time, though, there would be one big difference. This time Hector would stay close beside his mother. He had no desire to go off on another adventure.

About the Author

Jane Scoggins Bauld has dedicated her life to the well-being of young children. She is a Child Development expert, and has taught pre-kindergarten for thirty years, winning several teaching awards. She is a well-known Child Development speaker and consultant throughout Texas.

Through her first book, *Rights for Children*, Jane has worked diligently to improve the way children throughout the world are thought of and cared for. She visits schools regularly to read and talk to children.

Jane lives on a wooded acre in the rolling hills of northwest Austin with her husband Nathan, a professor of chemistry at The University of Texas, her cat Maui, and her yellow Labrador Quanah. They have five children and four grandchildren. Jane enjoys art history and wildflower identification.

For as long as he can remember, Gary Laronde has always loved to draw. He is a self-taught artist who has been influenced by the paintings of Renoir and Rockwell. His interest in illustrating children's books was sparked by watching "Reading Rainbow" with his young sons. Gary currently lives in Arlington, Texas, with his very supportive wife, Minnie, and his two wonderful sons, Brandon and Shane.